I'm Sorry Story

By Melody McAllister
Illustrated by Rheanna R. Longoria

I'm Sorry Story
by Melody McAllister
Published by EduMatch®
PO Box 150324, Alexandria, VA 22315

www.edumatch.org

sarah@edumatch.org

ISBN: 978-1-970133-49-3

DEDICATION

This book is dedicated to my children Madi, Ben, Lela,
Lizzie, and Whit and also to all of the my students
who've sat in my classroom or hugged me in the hallway.
Thanks to my friend, Todd Milbourn, for always being
willing to help me edit my writing! Thank you to my
husband, Mac, for believing in and supporting me!
Thank you Sarah & Mandy for taking a chance on me.
M.M.

To my husband, Adam
For your love and encouragement everyday; you are my
everything! R.L

The alarm clock was blaring. Ryan hit the snooze and slowly opened one eye, and as he stretched, he noticed the sun's rays illuminating his room through the blinds. The brightness reminded him of how it used to feel to run outside and jump into the puddles after the storms when he was younger. But then he reminded himself to get ready for school so he could eat breakfast before waiting at the bus stop. So he quickly dressed because he was always running behind!

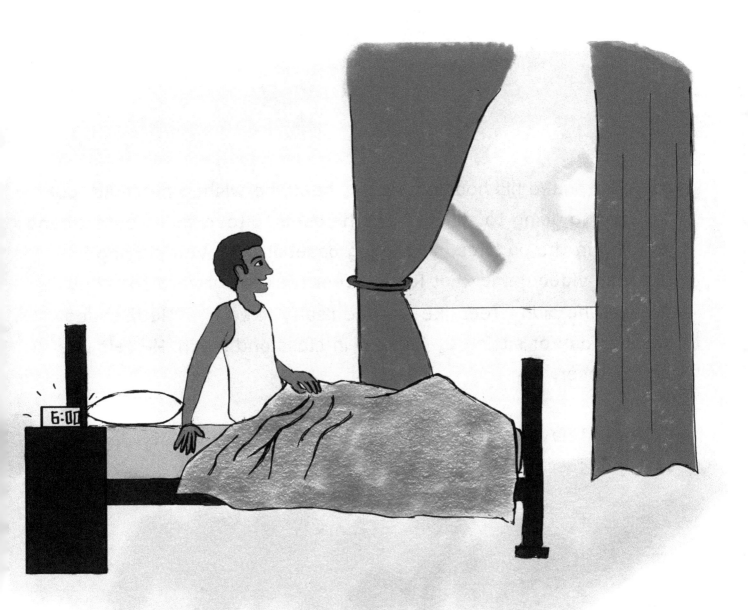

As Ryan pulled his hoodie over his head, he wished he could look forward to going to school—like he used to love going outside and jumping in the puddles, or playing baseball, or even playing his favorite video game...but Ryan never looked forward to school because he didn't feel like anyone really liked him. He dreaded another day of sitting by himself in class and lunch. He felt like such a loser.

At least *I have really cool shoes*, he thought to himself, as he tied up the laces.

It was normal for Ryan to be running late in the morning so he rushed to the kitchen to eat his breakfast. As he was throwing his dishes into the sink, he accidentally knocked his little sister's cereal on the floor. "Sorry," he muttered to her and ran out the door to catch his bus.

Ryan ran up to his bus stop. Two other kids were just about to get on when he, without even thinking, barged right in front of them. He didn't mean to make them mad, but he heard MacKenzie angrily whisper to Harley, "Ryan always cuts. Why does he always have to be first? We were the ones here waiting before he pushed us out of the way. I'm so sick of him!"

Ryan heard MacKenzie and turned to her from his seat and quietly said, "Sorry."

MacKenzie glared back at him and rolled her eyes. Ryan wondered why she was still mad at him? At home, his mom always made him say he was sorry and then everything was supposed to be okay....

Arriving at school, Ryan took his binder out of his backpack and was getting ready for first period math. One of the boys in his class was getting a detention write up for not doing this homework. This boy was **always** getting detention for not doing his homework. *When will he ever learn?* thought Ryan. He imagined Diego getting detention in college and giggled. Diego and Mrs. James looked over at him. "That's enough, Ryan," Mrs. James pointedly told him.

As he looked at Diego, he found an angry scowl staring back at him. "Sorry," Ryan responded.

Diego didn't say anything in return, and as always, Ryan was confused and wondered *why doesn't Diego just forgive him and get over it?*

After fourth period, Ryan hurried to be first in the lunch line because he was so hungry! He accidentally stepped on Julia's toes and before he could tell her he was sorry, Mrs. James sent him to the back of the line. "People are more important than being first, Ryan. We are all hungry. They were here first, so you need to go to the end of the line."

It was so hard for Ryan not to roll his eyes at the teacher, but as he looked at the others' irritated faces, he realized they were as "hangry" as him.

"Sorry, guys," he muttered as he found his spot at the end of the line. He felt frustrated because he hated being last. Being first felt so much better!

But Mrs. James' words got him thinking. He loved being first, but so did everyone else. Someone has to be first and someone has to be last. He still got his lunch, but he was going to have less time to play basketball before the next bell started fifth period.

There wasn't any recess in sixth grade, but they had a longer lunch time so they could go outside and play ball, or just talk. Ryan always felt stuck if he was last in line, so he hurriedly shoved his food in his mouth. The kids at his table gave him grossed-out looks. He glared at them, but they were already ignoring him again. He picked up his tray and sat at another table, alone.

After he finished eating, Ryan always played basketball. He was actually pretty good at it. Sometimes he was one of the last to be chosen for a team, but he tried to play every day.

Today, he wanted to show off what he'd been practicing, so he hustled to get every rebound possible. Sometimes he didn't have a great shot, but instead of passing the ball to his teammate, he repeatedly shot the ball where he was, even making a few!

Oddly, no one congratulated him, not even his own team! Ryan felt super-confused as he left the court.

Trey, who was in the seventh grade, saw how confused Ryan looked, so he explained, "Ryan, if you want to play basketball, you have to remember your teammates. This isn't one-on-one...you know you have five others on your team."

"Sorry," Ryan answered back as he walked away, feeling more lonely than he had at lunch.

He sat on a swing and whispered angrily to himself, "I worked so hard to show those guys how good I am. I made all of those shots. Why do I feel like I'm the loser? Trey missed two out of three times and everyone loves him!"

He didn't even notice when Mrs. James sat down on the swing next to him. "Ryan," she asked, "What's wrong?"

Ryan thought for a minute. He would like to talk to someone. He really didn't understand why he didn't have any friends, but it was embarrassing to talk about. He waited a while before answering.

"Mrs. James, I don't know why the other kids don't like me. I know sometimes I get in a hurry, and I know I'm not perfect, but my mom says that no one is perfect. I saw Harley pull Diego's hair yesterday at lunch. They cussed at each other and got in trouble, even. But today, they are friends again! Does anyone ever like me when I mess up? NO! I even tell them 'sorry!'"

Ryan didn't mean to get emotional but it all just came out of him in a rush! He'd been holding on to this hurt for a long time.

"Ryan, thank you so much for sharing this with me. I feel the pain you have. Would you like me to explain to you what is going on?" Ryan nodded.

Mrs. James continued, "Often, I only hear you say 'sorry.' When you apologize, you want the person you hurt to understand his feelings are important to you. When you apologize, you tell them, 'I'm sorry for not passing the ball to you.' You can't undo what you did to hurt someone, but you can try to make it right by admitting you were wrong. And then, Ryan, you offer a way to make the situation right. But when you blurt out the word 'sorry' and go on with whatever you are doing, the other person doesn't feel like you really meant your apology."

Silently, he considered all of Mrs. James' words. His brain felt overwhelmed! No one had ever taught him to apologize like that. He remembered the last time a boy in class tried to trip him. When the teacher made that boy apologize, "sorry" didn't make him feel any better! But he thought to himself, *I'm just doing what I thought was right.*

"Mrs. James, I was only doing what I thought was right, but I will try to apologize like you say. Do you think they'll accept me if I do it your way?"

Mrs. James could see that Ryan needed to be encouraged, "You are a really nice young man, Ryan. You are talented and very smart. I think if you start putting others first and taking responsibility for when you are wrong, you will see other students treat you better, too."

"Thank you, Mrs. James," Ryan replied. He sure hoped she was right as he walked home from the bus stop later that day. He would definitely give it a shot.

The next morning, Ryan woke up determined to make it a different kind of day. After eating his breakfast, he didn't rush up to put his bowl in the sink. First, he picked up his little sister's bowl before taking care of his own. He wanted to start his day by thinking of someone else before he thought of himself. Then, he thanked his mom for getting him the new clothes he was wearing! He knew by her surprised expression that he should have thanked her a long time ago. It seemed to do the trick.

His little sister and mom gave him huge smiles and hugs before he left for the bus stop. He realized that he really liked this feeling inside and was determined to keep putting others first.

As usual, he was running a little late to his stop and he saw the bus approaching and MacKenzie and Harley waiting in line. He was about to jump in, but changed his mind quickly and headed for the last spot. MacKenzie and Harley looked at him in confusion. Understanding what their expressions meant, Ryan told them, "MacKenzie and Harley, I'm sorry for cutting in front of the line before. I never even thought about how it made you feel. Will you forgive me?"

Even more confused, both girls nodded their heads and smiled at him. Ryan heard Harley whisper, "Maybe he isn't such a jerk like we thought!"

Later, when Diego was getting written up for not doing his homework, he automatically looked at Ryan, who'd laughed at him every day of that year. Ryan did not even pay attention when Diego received a detention warning.

After lunch, Ryan decided to apologize to Diego. He felt really nervous, but he knew what he needed to do. With all the courage he could muster, he walked right over to Diego and apologized for all the times he had laughed at him when he got in trouble.

With a shaky voice, he said, "Diego, man, I've laughed at you every day this year when Mrs. James gave you a detention. I know it made you mad and it was none of my business. If you ever need help in math, I can help after lunch or after school. I'm really sorry...do you...uhh...think you could...umm...forgive me?"

Diego, who was first surprised, then speechless, blinked a lot, but accepted his apology, "Dude, you've been a total jerk this year. I could never understand why you always laughed at me. I have to help out a lot with my younger siblings after school and I'm too tired to do the gazillion problems Mrs. James always assigns for homework! I know what I'm doing, sheesh! I wish she'd lay off, and I was really sick of you laughing, too. But yeah, I think I can forgive you. I'd rather finish math during lunch than in detention. And then we still have time to play ball."

Ryan let out a sigh of relief, and it came out like a whoosh! It gave him and Diego a good laugh and cleared the air between them. Ryan's relief turned into amazement when Diego picked him to be on his basketball team!

However, old habits take time to change. The very next day, Ryan was so excited at lunch, he ran in the cafeteria and elbowed his way to the front of the line. He ended up stepping on A'nia's toes and spilling Zaena's milk! Boy, was he in trouble. Mrs. James marched straight up to his mess and she didn't look happy! Ryan felt bad for his actions and immediately started apologizing.

"A'nia and Zaena, I am so sorry for rushing to the front of the line and stepping on your toes and spilling your milk. You were already in line and I shouldn't have tried to cut in front of you. I was wrong and I made a mess. I'm really sorry and I'll clean it up and get you a new milk. Will you please forgive me?"

Both girls had known Ryan for a long time and were amazed at his apology. Could this be the same Ryan they'd gone to school with for three years now?

Lost in their amazement, they forgot to speak until Mrs. James nudged them, "Girls?"

Finding their tongues, they both said, "That's okay, Ryan."

Mrs. James looked at the girls and Ryan, let out a deep breath, and began to lecture, "Actually," she began, and she moved her head to stare into each of their eyes to make sure they were listening, "it's not okay to run in the cafeteria and knock people over, but you CAN accept his apology." Everyone was glad her lecture was thirty seconds instead of five minutes! They understood her and took action before she continued.

The girls looked at each other, at Mrs. James, and then at Ryan before telling him, "Ryan, we accept your apology."

"Thank you, girls," said Mrs. James.

"Thank you, Zaena and A'nia," answered a relieved Ryan. Then he gave them some change to get new milk and cleaned up the mess he made.

At the end of the line, he was okay with being last. Zaena and A'nia weren't mad at him! He realized that changing wasn't super easy, but it was definitely worth the effort. He didn't feel like a loser at the back of the line because he was proud of himself for making things right.

As he left the line with his tray, Diego motioned him over to sit next to him and a few of his friends. This time Ryan was the happily speechless one — a hopeful idea of friendship came into his brain and he thought, "Yeah, it was definitely worth the effort!"

Discussion Questions

- How did Ryan change from the beginning of the story? Does he seem like anyone you know?

- Why didn't Diego respond when Ryan told him, "Sorry?"

- Have you ever felt like Ryan? When? Where?

- Have you ever felt like Diego or one of the other characters? When?

- How do you apologize to someone?

- What kind of advice would you give to Ryan or someone in your class about apologizing?

- Do you always have to forgive someone?

- Can you only forgive someone after they've apologized?

- If you do forgive someone, does it have to be right away?

- Why do you think Mrs. James didn't want the girls to say, "It's okay," to Ryan after he apologized?

- What events in your life popped into your head when you were listening to this story?

- Do you need to make time to apologize to someone today?

- Do you wish someone would apologize to you for something they did to you?

- What can you do to show you are putting others before yourself?

Follow Up Activities

Read at Circle Time or Class Meeting and allow students to reflect on a time where an apology helped and when it hurt. What was the difference? Let them choose how they want to express their story (orally, written, creative writing app, illustration, poem, etc.).

Write a play and perform it about working through a problem with another person.

Make a step-by-step poster of a sincere apology.

Illustrate a bookmark to be laminated and handed out about sincere apologies.

Use an acronym to help remember how to apologize with a sincere heart.

Write the author and tell her your thoughts about the story!

Melody McAllister

PO Box 140547 Anchorage, AK 99514

About the Author

Melody McAllister is a wife, mom of five, and educator. She and her family recently moved from Texas to Alaska to live a new adventure! She graduated from Southeastern Oklahoma State University and began teaching in 2004. She loves to write and finds inspiration from her faith, children, students, and life in general.

McAllister received the 2017 Garland NAACP Educator of the Year. She is a contributing author for other books such as Mandy Froehlich's <u>The Fire Within</u> and <u>EduMatch Snapshot in Education 2019</u>. She is also the Logistics Manager for EduMatch Publishing.

If you are a teacher or parent and would like to set up a virtual author storytime, please contact Melody McAllister at melody@mjmcalliwrites.com

Find her on Twitter @mjmcalli and her website mjmcalliwrites.com Follow her blog HeGaveMeAMelody.com

EduMatch Publishing

CPSIA information can be obtained
at www.ICGtesting.com
Printed in the USA
BVHW050041261121
622404BV00007B/74